For B.P-H. and my gorgeous Tom, Rafi & Gabe,
YOU are my sunshine - S.P-H. x x x x

For JB, and for best friends big and small xx - A.B.

BLOOMSBURY CHILDREN'S BOOKS
Bloomsbury Publishing Plc
50 Bedford Square, London, WC1B 3DP, UK

BLOOMSBURY, BLOOMSBURY CHILDREN'S BOOKS and the Diana logo are trademarks of Bloomsbury Publishing Plc

First published in Great Britain by Bloomsbury Publishing Plc

A catalogue record for this book is available from the British Library

978 1 4088 7896 5 (HB)
978 1 4088 7895 8 (PB)
978 1 4088 7894 1 (eBook)

2 4 6 8 10 9 7 5 3 1

Printed in China by Leo Paper Products, Heshan, Guangdong

All papers used by Bloomsbury Publishing Plc are natural, recyclable products from
wood grown in well managed forests. The manufacturing processes conform to
the environmental regulations of the country of origin.

To find out more about our authors and books visit www.bloomsbury.com and sign up for our newsletters

You Make Me Happy

Smriti Prasadam-Halls   Alison Brown

BLOOMSBURY
CHILDREN'S BOOKS
LONDON OXFORD NEW YORK NEW DELHI SYDNEY

You make me happy,
you make me sing.

There's a bounce in my footstep,
like bunnies in spring.

You make me happy,
like birds taking flight.
Like a waterfall twinkling,
like morning's first light.

The things that you do, and the things that you say,
fill me with sunshine and brighten my day.

You're so full of wonder. I'm full of surprise.
We see things afresh through each other's eyes.

You show me the fun
in whatever we find.

We know we look silly
but hey, we don't mind!

You love to be cheeky, you know that you do . . .

but I can't seem to *ever* stay grumpy with you.

Whenever you hug me, so tight and so sweet,
my toes start to tingle, my heart skips a beat.

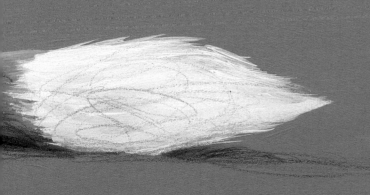

When the going gets tough and life makes me frown,
when my heart starts to sink like the sun going down . . .

you bring back the sunshine and out of the blue,
you make me laugh with the things that you do.

I find that I'm giggling, I find that I'm glad,
I find that I'm smiling, no time to be sad.

And when I look into
your bright, sparkly eyes,
there's a song in my heart,
there are stars in the skies.

You make me happy,
you make me new.
Together there's NOTHING
that we cannot do.

You make me happy and hopeful and strong . . .

. . . and right by your side
is where I belong.